THIS BOOK BELONGS TO

· ·

Our society today is increasingly sensitive to two diverse but related issues—child abuse and animal care. Jane Nord has created a masterful work in *Paranoia: A Cat's Tale* by engaging both the adult and child mind at the same time. This creation should be in every child's [and parent's] library as a reminder that understanding, love, and compassion are essential if the helpless are to experience security and happiness in a world that often dispenses pain and disappointment. Jane Nord has hit the mark with this engaging tale and will delight young and old alike with her gift of insight and expressing.

—Clinton L. Schultz, MDiv, MS, NCC,
Christian Counseling Northwest

Paranoia: A Cat's Tale resonates with poetic imagery, enthralling to children, yet easily enjoyed by adults as well. Any victim of abuse will find solace in Paranoia's tale. Life choices and discipline needn't be abusive. Patience, tenderness, and acceptance are salves shared with Paranoia during a healing process. I hope this book will be in every school library and hopefully added to the *Accelerated Reader* test list used in many schools.

—Trudy Weston,
Educator and Librarian, Cheney, Washington

Published by Tate Publishing & Enterprises, LLC
127 E. Trade Center Terrace | Mustang, Oklahoma 73064 USA
1.888.361.9473 | www.tatepublishing.com

Tate Publishing is committed to excellence in the publishing industry. The company reflects the philosophy established by the founders, based on Psalm 68:11,
"The Lord gave the word and great was the company of those who published it."

Book design copyright © 2008 by Tate Publishing, LLC. All rights reserved.
Cover design & interior design by Elizabeth A. Mason
Illustrations by Genevieve Stotler

Published in the United States of America
ISBN: 978-1-60696-611-2
1. Juvenile Non-Fiction: Rhyme: Ages 4-8: Animals: Cats
2. Juvenile Non-Fiction: Social Situations: Abandonment: Abuse
08.08.18

PaRaNoIa

A Cat's Tale

JANE NORD

TATE PUBLISHING & *Enterprises*

DEDICATION

To the small children and animals of the
earth that can't speak for themselves.

ACKNOWLEDGEMENT

To my friends who read, counseled, and encouraged; my dad
who believed; and my husband, John, the computer man.
Thank you!

FOREWORD

Jane has a heart that cares for children and animals who have been wounded emotionally and physically. As I read Paranoia's story, the lines and rhymes rolled off my tongue and I knew its message was a gift. If a generation of children can be taught the value of treating animals with dignity, perhaps as adults they will champion the cause of ending neglect and abuse. Jane has succeeded wonderfully in speaking for those who cannot speak for themselves.

—Beth Morrill,
mother, teacher, licensed midwife

I want to tell you a story as seen through my cat eyes.
The story is so awesome; I'm glad there are no lies.
In the beginning things were very good.
We spent lazy days as little kittens should.

I was on one side; on the other was Tommy,
As we curled up with our loving mommy.
When I got bigger, I saw things to do;
I didn't know the curtains were new.

The food on the table was very tasty;
The bird in the cage should not go to wastey.
Tommy and I had curled up for a nap,
When in came the man and closed our box flap.

We were *afraid* and called out in despair;
Our mommy couldn't hear us inside of there.
The man dropped us off we didn't know where,
Then he drove away...

GETTING RID OF HIS CARE.

The long night came and we were alone.
Where was our mommy and our happy home?
When morning came we saw a mouse,
Going down the trail toward his own house.

Tommy was quick just like a lion.
I was so hungry I thought I was dyin.'
He had his breakfast and it was good,
When he hissed at me I understood.

He caught the mouse and cats don't share.
I'd soon be dead, and he didn't care!
So I sat on a mound in the cold, wet air.
The rain came down and matted my hair.

Out of the corner of my eye I saw
A hungry coyote and his racing paw.
My legs launched me into the air,
But hungry coyote was already there.

HE SHOOK ME, TRYING TO BREAK ME IN HALF;
From his mouth came a hideous laugh.
My claws sunk deep into his nose;
Then out of his grip this cat arose.

In that moment he let go of his prey,
I flew up a tree and I got away.
Coyote growled and snarled as he waited below.
He finally left; he had somewhere to go.

Down the tree I went with *pain* in my back,
My legs wouldn't work; they were all out of whack.
One day a car stopped and people got out.
"Would they be kind?" I had reason to doubt.

We were afraid and began to run;
Tommy was fast and got ahead some.
He went to a place where they didn't see.
Because I was injured I couldn't flee.

I HISSED at the man and showed him my claws;
He wasn't afraid of disobeying cat laws.
By the nape of the neck he had me caught,
Even though I was hurt I really fought.

He put me in the car and we went for a ride.
When we got to his house, he took me inside.
An old lady named Gram was visiting there.
"Who could have done this?" she said with care.

She scooped me up and took me away;
I'd be her little cat if she had her say.
With bony long fingers, she made up my bed,
"You look pretty bad," was all that she said.

A bowl of cat food with chunks of meat,
Feelin' so poorly that I couldn't eat.

When evening came, canned food was for dinner.
I tasted the gravy; it was a winner.

Gram often visited in the days that would follow.
How could she know that my heart was hollow?
And what was Gram telling me?
She said, "You're stinky but shouldn't be."

With water and soap she filled up the tub,
Then put me in and started to scrub.
My claws came out; I was ready to fight.
She grabbed my legs and held me down tight.

She washed me and cleaned me and gave me a wink.
With all of that washing I thought I would shrink.
After my bath we rocked in her chair;
I began to relax and found comfort there.

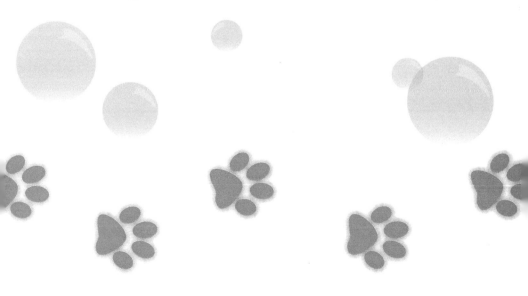

Purr

Purr

Purr

In those happy moments I forgot all my trouble,
Then out of my throat purring did bubble.
Gram talked to me she wouldn't fib,
She said, "You are thin, I see every rib."

Gram gave me medicine and it was icky;
It dripped down my face making me sticky.
After three weeks I began to recover,
Walking around on legs made of rubber.

The shower curtain I had to climb,
And plenty of toilet paper I could unwind.
Each day I could see Gram as she did the dishes.
To be my best friend was one of her wishes.

Often she would carry me down the hall.
I'd hurry for the bathroom and the back of the stall.
Gram said "Paranoia" would be my name,
Hiding in the bathroom would be my fame.

One day Gram had had quite enough,
Finding some string tied me up with the stuff.
A little short leash that wasn't too long,
I could hardly move it had to be wrong.

I jumped and I pulled and I almost flipped,
I kept on trying until I was whipped.
After a while I settled down,
Sitting under the chair wearing a frown.

Gram worked in the kitchen, she cleaned the house,
I was tied to my chair and I saw a mouse.
I jumped one foot, that was not very long,
The sneaky mouse had sung his last song.

Gram was impressed to say the least,
As I ate up that little mouse beast.
Then I became content under my chair,
Not having a tether to hold me there.

Gram started saying I should venture outside,
So I began planning where I would hide.
Gram would call out, "It will cause you no pain,"
She opened the door and I saw all the rain.

I hissed at the dog, "Oh what a brat,"
'Cause I'm just a helpless little pussy cat.
With Gram's big foot, she pushed me out the door.
"I can't be outside!" I said with a little cat roar.

Then I began learning how to get along,
To scratch at the dog would be very wrong.
That's when I thought I could eat with the dog.
Did you know that the dog was a hog?

I'd play in the hay and I'd take a nap,
I'd climb up a tree without a mishap.
Gram picked up the phone and made a phone call.
I have an appointment, it's useless to stall.

I'm going to the vet; I'll be spayed today,
When I get home I won't want to play.
After a few days I will recover.
I'll have a good life with Gram,

'cause I love her.

e|LIVE

listen|imagine|view|experience

AUDIO BOOK DOWNLOAD INCLUDED WITH THIS BOOK!

In your hands you hold a complete digital entertainment package. Besides purchasing the paper version of this book, this book includes a free download of the audio version of this book. Simply use the code listed below when visiting our website. Once downloaded to your computer, you can listen to the book through your computer's speakers, burn it to an audio CD or save the file to your portable music device (such as Apple's popular iPod) and listen on the go!

How to get your free audio book digital download:

1. Visit www.tatepublishing.com and click on the e|LIVE logo on the home page.
2. Enter the following coupon code:
   50c0-2161-73ec-c22a-4ec1-235a-0cd6-e533
3. Download the audio book from your e|LIVE digital locker and begin enjoying your new digital entertainment package today!